The House of Horrors

Halloween Madness - Book 2

A Starlight Investigation Short Story

Marnie Atwell

ISBN: 978-0-6450281-4-0

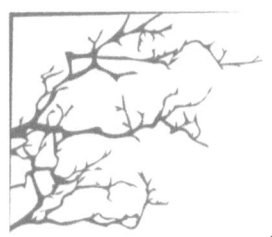

Chapter One

After scrubbing the walls of Force's room in the pub to remove the graphics drawn by a very naughty pencil, the team was ready for a shower. April escorted Briella to their room next door while Force and Scout headed to a stream he had discovered a week ago.

"This is lovely," Scout exclaimed, inspecting the delicate yellow flowers poking through the rockery.

"I thought you would like it," he smiled, removing his shirt and placing it over a boulder. Force waded into the water until his black board shorts were covered. "The shallowest part seems to be over there," he pointed to an inlet in the landscape behind him. "It is perfectly scaled for a fairy who prefers natural baths to chemically laced ones."

Scout grinned as she flew over his head to reach the area he'd pointed out. "I don't know how

Briella's skin has remained as healthy as it has with the chlorine and fluoride that's been added to the water supply she uses in her bath."

"I guess it's what her body has become accustomed to. I hope she doesn't develop any skin conditions by changing over to rainwater from the tank," he stated with concern. Force hadn't even considered her primary needs may not be met by the new arrangement. "April is plumbing two tanks into your new house. One to provide an inflow into the house and one to capture the outflow. Perhaps I can suggest she add chemicals to the tank to emulate town water. That way, Briella will be using water similar to what she is used to."

Scout slid into the water with a sigh of pleasure. "This is so good," she groaned moving in a little deeper. She stripped out of her top and pants and threw them onto the bank. She wasn't concerned about getting redressed. Force was ever the gentleman and would leave to give her privacy when she was ready. "I think that is a good idea. I would prefer to swim and bathe somewhere like this than in a bathtub enclosed by four walls."

THE HOUSE OF HORRORS

"What if I was to install a swimming pool or spa in the fairy garden? Which would you want to use then?"

That got Scout's attention. She hadn't considered that as an option. "I'd have to say I could put up with town water if it was in that sort of setting. I can always swim here, but I doubt I could ever convince Briella to try it. I think she might be a germaphobe."

"Really?" Force replied with a tinge of surprise.

"Have you ever seen a speck of dirt on her for more than a few seconds?"

"She seemed to manage okay at the pumpkin patch last night."

"True," Scout replied, breaking into a breast-stroke. Force dipped his head below the water and rubbed his hands over his face. "There are some turtles in this river. Be careful where you swim," he warned.

"I'll stay in this pool of water when I come for a swim. There is a ridge between my section and yours that will give me warning of any uninvited guests."

3

"You won't be tempted to swim in the deeper section if your water evaporates?"

"No. If there's no water here, I'll swim in the pool or laze in the spa. Whichever you choose to include in the fairy garden."

"I might put in both. I think Briella is more likely to·use the spa so we could fill that up with the chemically treated tank water. The pool can be yours, filled with natural rainwater. I would need to add a waterfall so there is a continuous flow of water to keep the pool clean. A small pump run on solar power to keep the water moving up to the top of the waterfall would work. Hmmm, I really like this idea."

"She can swim in it if she wants to," Scout said, her tone defensive on behalf of her friend.

"Of course. Just like you can use the spa if you wish to," Force explained. "The objects won't be exclusively owned. The fairy garden and all things included will be jointly owned."

Scout nodded her head, pleased by the direction of their conversation. They fell into a comfortable silence. She had paddled around for fifteen minutes before tiring of the activity. She felt recharged physically, but mentally the nagging feeling that Briella's magic was going to strike again was strengthening. Scout found out only yesterday that Briella has problems with her magic every year in the time leading up to Halloween. It is usually only a couple of days, but this year, her problems started ten days before Halloween.

Scout tried to calm herself, but her mind refused to focus on something else. She didn't want to ruin Force's morning, but with their friendship being so close, he picked up on her antsy vibes without her saying a word. "What's wrong, Scout? Are you worried about Briella?"

"Not worried about her so much as what her magic is capable of," Scout admitted. "I've got this terrible feeling, Force. Worse is yet to come."

"Don't sweat it, Scout. April has everything under control for now. You cannot take on the responsibility of ensuring Briella remains magic free until the first of November. She either will or won't be able to prevent further incidents of mayhem. All we can do is provide her with our support and to fill up her days with enjoyable experiences that don't require magic. If something does go awry, we will be there to lend a hand. April and I can always modify memories of anybody who learns more than they should."

"I guess," Scout said unhappily, floating on her front with head out of the water and both hands touching the bottom of the pond. Her black underwear looked like a bikini. "What do you think she is doing at the moment, Force?"

"Briella is happily occupied. No need to concern yourself," he caged not giving a straight answer. This immediately put Scout's back up. Force only said things like that when he thought she wouldn't like the answer.

"What aren't you telling me?" she demanded gruffly, entirely out of character. Usually, when she wanted to get information from him, her tone became as sweet as honey. She had definitely used the wrong tactic, the pitch of her voice put him on the defensive.

"Why do you think I am hiding something?" he countered a tad aggressively.

"I have my reasons," she spluttered indignantly. Taking a deep breath to calm herself, she wondered why she was upset in the first place. Scout realised she was a little jealous that Force knew what was going on back at the pub and she didn't. Briella was supposed to be her best friend, but so was Force. In fact, Scout was closer to him than she was to Briella. "I'm sorry, Force. I didn't mean to snap."

"I know, Scout. All is well," he said quietly.

"Can you give me a hint?"

"I'm going to have to replace your spare pouch of special pencils," he confessed.

"You needn't bother," Scout said in a relieved voice. She hadn't known what to expect, but it definitely hadn't been that. "I'm not very good at drawing things, and Briella is extremely talented. Those pencils are kind of wasted on colouring in, which is mainly what I use them for. I probably would have given them to her anyway. I've got a few projects in mind for her to design."

"Oh, really?" he asked intrigued.

"Yep!" she grinned.

Force let it drop, knowing she was baiting him as payback for earlier. "Do you want to see what she's been up to?"

"That would be great," Scout replied.

"Give me a second, and I'll leave you to get dressed."

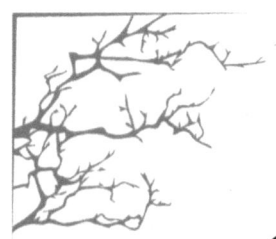

Chapter Two

Briella's bath was short and to the point. There wasn't a lot of joy to the experience when the surroundings consisted of a fairy-sized tent. The window of her bathroom back at the apartment overlooked a gorgeous selection of fake plants in planter boxes. Briella looked forward to being able to use the new bathroom in her new holiday house, overlooking a real fairy garden.

Dressed in a red tank top and a pair of black shorts, she pulled her hair into a ponytail and scowled at the reflection of her emerald coloured eyes in the mirror. "Someone could have mentioned my eyes didn't match my outfit," she grumbled, having worn a black and red jumpsuit the previous day.

"There were more important things going on than the colour of your irises, Briella," April said, thinking about the overnight stay in the pumpkin patch where four pumpkins had been accidently animated by Briella's wonky magic. Briella flopped onto the middle cushion of a three seater sofa located on the coffee table in the living area. She flicked the ponytail over the back of the chair to prevent it from becoming pinned between herself and the seat.

"What's the matter, Briella?"

"I'm bored already. How am I supposed to cope with sitting around all day doing nothing? I am not going to survive the next nine days if I can't do anything exciting in case I use my magic."

"Who said you have to sit around being bored?"

"No-one," Briella admitted. "I just thought it was what you all wanted."

"We all want to see you happy and having fun. It would be preferable if you didn't use your magic and cause mayhem. If your joy should happen to bring other things to life, we'll deal with it." Briella tried to cut in, but April wouldn't let her. "Don't let what might happen stop you from living your life, Briella."

THE HOUSE OF HORRORS

"What am I supposed to do? We got lucky with the pumpkins. Imagine if the trouble had have happened on a larger scale."

"It didn't," April answered.

"Imagine if it did," Briella insisted, continuing on her worst case scenario theme.

"I have something for you," April grinned in anticipation of her reaction.

"What is it?" Briella asked with little enthusiasm.

"Oh, you could at least pretend to be excited, for my benefit. Way to kill my buzz."

"Sorry, April. It's hard to feel enthusiastic when I know what it could lead to."

"Then I guess you won't be interested in this," April declared, pulling an upside-down shoe box off a gift hidden beneath.

Briella sucked in a breath of surprise. She leapt to her feet and raced over to the object. It was a room without a ceiling, and the doorway was facing her. Briella glanced at April, quietly seeking permission to enter. April's grin widened as she nodded her head. She peered over the top as Briella raced through the doorway.

"This is an art studio for your new house, Briella. Liam and I thought you might like to use it before your home is assembled.

"You've been building my house in parts?" she asked, raising her eyebrows at April's affirming nod. Briella glanced around the room, liking the pale grey walls and the linoleum flooring that looked like white tiles. A bay window was built into the wall opposite the doorway, which had a white window seat and peach curtains pulled across the glass. Pride of place, though, was a stool and easel made from polished wood. Lying across the top was a sketch pad and a pouch filled with Scout's special pencils.

"April, this is beautiful, but you shouldn't have taken Scout's pencils. They are professional artist quality and extremely expensive."

"It's okay, Briella. Force gave them to me. He knows a guy who will replace them for a bit above cost price. I thought you might like to sketch some pictures for your new house."

12

THE HOUSE OF HORRORS

Briella sat on the stool then flipped the cloth to reveal the colours inside. "Ooh, these are the deluxe edition," she breathed with awe.

"Are they?" April leaned in for a closer look.

"Yep! Can you grab the piece of paper underneath the glass container over there? The one shaped like a leaf."

April reached over and retrieved the picture Briella had drawn the day before. There were two sketches on the sheet. One was a witch's costume and the other was a long-sleeved jumpsuit with cat's tail and a hood with cat's ears attached. It appeared to be covered in fur.

"This is really good, Briella," April said, admiring the detail of the sketch.

"Do you think you could make them for Scout and me before Halloween? We would like to have a little fun in our new house by dressing up on All Hallows' Eve."

"I think I can manage that." April scanned the artwork more closely. "Do you want me to make a face mask for the cat?"

"No, I think I would get too scared with something over my face on Halloween. I might just use a bit of makeup and draw on a cat's face. Do you think you could get me some pipe cleaners or fishing line for the whiskers?"

"Absolutely," April replied. "It would be my pleasure."

"Instead of drawing pictures for my house right now, do you think I could draw some spooky pictures for our party instead?" Briella was thinking about all of the things Scout had envisioned for a surprise party for April and Liam. Scout had asked her to draw the props for the gathering, and she would use her magic to make them come off the paper into a 3D object as Briella's magic was on the fritz.

"You can use the paper and pencils for whatever you like. Let me know when you are running low so I can restock them for you."

"Thanks, April."

"Do you need anything else?"

"No, I'm good, thank you. I really appreciate this, April," Briella answered, lifting the cover of the pad

14

and tucking it behind the cardboard on the back. She took a pale grey pencil out of the case and began to sketch the outline of a skeleton. It was dark enough to see what she was doing, yet, light enough to erase any mistakes she might make, easily.

As she worked, her tongue poked out on the left side of her mouth. She shaded the bones with varying strengths of cream and browns until it appeared like a miniature version of a real person's skeleton lying on her paper.

Once her picture was complete, Briella grabbed the black and began to draw a cloak over the top. The effect when she was finished was chilling. She shoved the end of the pencil in her mouth and clenched softly with her teeth. It needed something. The palm of the hand reaching towards her looked fine. It was the other one that seemed to be missing something. Briella picked out a red, a silver and a brown pencil then began alternating them as she worked her vision. When she was finished, she grinned with a wickedness worthy of an evil queen. The scythe dripping blood was a perfect accessory for a grim reaper who had turned rogue.

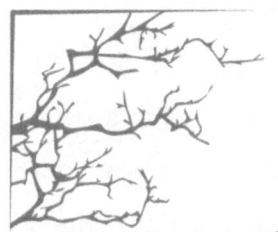

Chapter Three

Briella was mighty pleased with herself. She considered duplicating the picture a couple of times but decided her time was better spent bringing other ghoulish nightmares to life, pun not intended.

She grabbed some more shades of brown and got to work. In a couple of minutes, she had an outline of a werewolf. It stood on its hind legs, the front paws reaching to ensnare its victim. The wolf's head was thrown back, howling at a full moon that had yet to be drawn, it's teeth freakishly long and sharp. As always, the detail Briella put into her drawing was devastatingly good. Half an hour later the picture was finished right down to the cuticles of the claws.

Flipping over to a new page, Briella started to draw a vampire. She was basing her picture on the most famous of them all. No, not Edward Cullen, from the Twilight Saga, but Sarina: Queen of the Vampires on the planet, Mystique. Briella's likeness to the creature was uncanny. She drew her as she appeared to Briella, grotesque and evil. As she was female, she had never witnessed the alluring image that males saw when they gazed upon her flesh.

This drawing was going to take quite a bit longer. Briella was only a quarter of the way through the shading when Scout and Liam came into April's room. Scout couldn't contain her curiosity and flew right over the top of the wall and in through the ceiling.

"This is gorgeous," Scout exclaimed looking around. "Is this part of your house?"

"Our house, Scout. This is our new art studio."

"Wow, it has a nice feeling to it, doesn't it? Soothing to the soul."

"Yeah."

"Are all the rooms like this?"

"I don't know. I didn't ask April."

"We'll find out soon enough," Scout shrugged. "What have you been drawing?"

"You know about your pencils?"

Taking a note out of Briella's book, Scout waved her hand dismissively. "Don't worry about it. I would have given them to you anyway. A talent like yours can't go to waste. So let's see what you've been using it for."

Briella opened the sketchpad to the beginning and showed her the reaper and werewolf. Scout was ecstatic. "These are going to make fantastic props to scare our guests with." Scout turned the page to see what Briella was currently working on. She gasped with surprise. "Is that . . . "

"Yeah. It's Sarina."

"Do you think that's a good idea?" Scout answered with a quiver in her voice.

"I felt compelled to draw her and Toren. It has nothing to do with the party. I think I need to create a shrine to Toren and a reminder of what happened to him. I'll make sure the picture is not seen by anyone else."

"Perhaps you should finish it when the house is completed, and Force and April don't have a chance to see," Scout suggested.

"See what?" Force asked walking over.

"Nothing," Briella answered with fear of getting caught. She ripped out the page and looked for somewhere to hide it. Too late. Force had already spotted it. "What do you have there?"

"A picture of no importance. It's not very good."

"I doubt that. Hand it over," he held out his palm expectantly.

"I'd rather not," Briella mumbled, afraid he would become angry.

"Okay," Force replied. "But don't leave it lying around if you don't want others to see it."

"I won't," Briella brightened, tucking the picture into the back of the sketchpad. She would find somewhere to store it later until their house was ready and she could complete it in private.

"Am I allowed to see your other drawings?" he inquired.

"Sure," she smiled, showing him.

"That's an interesting assortment for hanging throughout your house."

"I decided to draw some pictures for Halloween. April and I celebrate every year. This year I thought I would celebrate with Scout in our new home."

"Interesting theme for a housewarming."

"A what?" Briella and Scout asked together.

"A party to welcome occupants to their new home. It's supposed to bring the owners good fortune."

"Oh," Briella said.

"Do we need to do that?"

"It's not mandatory, girls. Just a human tradition and as your existence is forbidden to be shared with the humans, a housewarming could only be performed with Gatherers and Locator fairies present."

"I think we'll give it a miss, no offence to you or April, and continue with the plan for the Halloween party," Briella said.

"As you wish. I need to get to town. Loretta wants me to take a look at a second-hand car she's looking to purchase."

"Are you two dating now?" Briella asked.

"No, we are just friends."

THE HOUSE OF HORRORS

"She kissed you when we were in the process of locating her daughter, Calamity, when she went missing," Scout scowled. "You seemed to enjoy it, immensely."

"Loretta just wants an honest opinion from somebody trustworthy," he frowned.

"She doesn't know you very well, does she?" Briella and Scout smirked at one another.

"What are you trying to say?" he laughed in an attempt to hide the feeling of hurt Briella's words brought him.

Scout narrowed her eyes, not the least bit fooled by his laughter. "What colour are your eyes, Force?" she asked.

"Brown," he replied as they changed from coral to a milk chocolate colour.

The fairies giggled sweetly. "You might be trustworthy in matters of great importance to humans, but you're not too reliable in keeping the secrets of the Starlight team under wraps. Imagine what the humans would do if they discovered your abilities, Liam."

"You are right, Briella. Catch up with you later. Stay out of trouble."

"Always," Scout replied.

"Hmmm, yeah right," he said, looking at Briella who scowled and turned to a fresh page on her sketchpad.

"What are you going to draw now?" Scout asked.

"I don't know. How about skeletons coming out of plots in front of their gravestones?"

"Don't forget the trap doors."

"Oh, yeah."

It took Briella an hour to draw three in a row. She illustrated them in landscape with Scout offering suggestions along the way. She wanted to ask Scout to be quiet and let her design them her own way, but she didn't. Briella didn't want to hurt Scout's feelings, and it was Scout's imagination that had brought about the party idea in the first place. She knew Scout was jealous of her ability to create a picture from nothing. It would be extremely frustrating for Briella to be able to see an image in her head and not be able to replicate it. That was how Scout felt. The problem was, Scout wasn't that great at describing what she saw, so the picture didn't appear how either of them envisioned it.

Scout realised after Briella had drawn the second gravestone and skeleton that their collaborative efforts weren't working. She resigned herself to having props that she wanted but not necessarily appearing how she imagined. After the last was completed, Scout also discovered it didn't really matter. Briella was a very competent drawer and when left to her own imagination, designed stunning artwork. Sometimes even better than what Scout had pictured.

Once Briella was finished with the page she took a break. She stretched her back muscles and grabbed a bit of orange juice April had squeezed into a tiny jug. She poured two glasses and proposed a toast. "To my best friend, Scout. May our hunt for creatures one day be over."

"Here, here," Scout replied, raising her glass.

"What are you going to work on next?"

"I thought we could have a haunted house for our display."

"That sounds awesome."

"Wait until you see it. The house is going to scare your pants off," Briella said, wiggling her fingers in front of Scout's face.

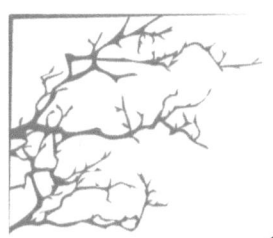

Chapter Four

Scout went to the cupboard and grabbed a small plate to put some mushroom on. Briella would be busy for a while and most likely be so absorbed in her task, she would forget to eat. She barely received a thank you as Scout dragged the lounge suite into the room with the plate sliding precariously across the cushion.

"April should put a small table in here for you to place your snacks and drinks on," Scout muttered.

"I shouldn't be eating in here, anyway," Briella responded, reaching for a black pencil.

"So, you would stop drawing to eat and drink?"

"Probably not," Briella admitted, knowing she forgot to complete mundane tasks when the creative bug took hold.

"I guess I'll leave you to it, then."

"What will you do?" Briella reached for a white highlighter.

"I don't know. I'll find something to occupy my time with."

"Come and see me in a few hours. I should be nearly finished by then."

"It's going to take you three hours to draw a box?"

"Oh, Scout. It will be much more than a box. By the time I'm finished, and you use your magic, this house will be two stories high with multiple rooms inside."

"How are you going to do that?"

"I'm going to draw the picture in layers. That way it won't be just an empty husk when it becomes a 3D model."

"I think it's going to take you more than three hours to do that."

"Hmm, more than likely," Briella agreed. "Come and see me anyway. I will probably need a good stretch by then. Out of curiosity, do you have more pencils stashed anywhere?"

"The set that I've been using can be found beneath Force's bed. They should be between half to three-quarters in length."

"Great!" Briella grinned, looking back at her drawing.

Scout left her to it and went in search of April. She found her sitting at the bar downstairs, holding a glass of water with a slice of lemon. Scout didn't want to interrupt her conversation with Robbie, the grandfatherly publican, but April felt Scout's presence and switched to speaking with mind-link.

'Everything okay, Scout?"

'Yes. Briella is busy drawing and will be occupied for a few hours.'

'Damn!' April's response surprised Scout.

'I thought you wanted her busy?' Scout replied.

'I do,' April responded to Scout before answering a comment Robbie made. She pulled a phone out of her pocket and viewed the screen. "I'm sorry, Robbie. I've got to head out. Raincheck?"

"Sure, love. Everything all right?"

"Yeah. I just need to check in with my boss in the city. I'll be back before dinner." She stood up and tucked the barstool beneath the overhang of the countertop.

"Want me to pack you a lunch basket?"

April smiled, "That won't be necessary, but thanks anyway."

"I'll have a steak ready for you at seven."

"That would be lovely. Will it accompany your world famous mashed veg with onion gravy?"

"Absolutely," he tipped his finger to his temple in salute.

"You're a gem," April threw over her shoulder. Scout fluttered from the railing post she had hidden behind to eye level as April approached the staircase. "Do you think Briella will be safe here for a few hours by herself?"

"Sure," Scout replied with a frown, feeling anxious over the reason April had asked.

"We haven't been near the city in almost two weeks, and I need to make sure there aren't any creatures causing havoc. I'd like to limit Briella's interactions within human areas in case her magic brings something to life.

"Quite understandable," Scout said, realising where the conversation was going. "You want me to come with you, instead."

"Yes. It will be just this once," April said. Scout raised her eyebrows.

"Okay," April said. "Maybe twice. We should probably check again in a few days' time. I shouldn't have let it go this long. Luckily, nothing seems to have surfaced on Starlight's radar."

"I guess you and Briella would be in a lot of trouble if a creature appeared and she wasn't there to detect it."

"Yes, we would."

"Do they know you are purchasing a holiday house with Force?"

"Yes. I have informed them. They know you and Force are making this your permanent residence. They have reorganised the boundaries with the other Locator Fairies to ensure there aren't any gaps. Everyone seems to be happy with the new arrangements."

"What about you and Briella?"

"They have demanded that we spend no more than a couple of days together with you and Liam. They have informed us that when Briella and I are here on a holiday break, you and Liam are to take over our apartment to watch over the people in our area," she replied.

"I see," Scout scowled. She wouldn't get to live with Briella after all, and she would be forced to spend Briella's holiday along the coastline, a place she hated with a passion. "Is Briella aware of these conditions?"

"No. I didn't want to upset her when her magic isn't working properly. I am sure we can work something out. Even if it means travelling a few hours every day or two to keep an eye on things back home when we take a holiday."

Scout perched on April's shoulder for the remainder of the trip upstairs.

"That defeats the purpose of a holiday, April. The whole idea is to relax, and not be running backwards and forwards."

April agreed but she had always kept herself busy anyway, and there wasn't a lot for her to do in the country. "You have noticed the sudden spike in cases, haven't you, Scout?"

"Yes, I have heard there have been more than usual."

"We can't afford for one to get a foothold here on Earth," April stated.

"No, we can't," Scout agreed. April opened the door to her place and moved to a suitcase on the ground near a double bed. She pulled out the battle suit, a unique piece of clothing that transformed to meet her needs. Scout flew off April's shoulder and sat on a pillow. She faced away from April while she got changed. "Did Briella tell you we have a wood nymph living in our forest?"

"No," April exclaimed, her tone rising in surprise.

"Her name is Dynopiah. She says 'The Purge' is nearly upon us."

"Really? That explains a lot," April's voice was thoughtful as though things that had bugged her were starting to fall into place. "Did she indicate a timeframe?" April inquired.

"One to two decades," Scout answered.

"Hmmm," April murmured. "Have you told Force?"

"No, not yet."

"Why not? Don't you think it is important?"

"Briella and I found out only yesterday and things sort of got complicated with the pumpkin patch."

"That's understandable. We might make a trip into the hinterlands on our return trip. I would like to see if Wynomiah is also awake from her slumber."

"Wynomiah?" Scout squeaked. "Is she a wood nymph, too? I thought they were extinct."

"No, they are not extinct, Scout. They only come out of their resting place when the world is in great peril."

"The world or the humans?"

"Now that the humans have made themselves the superior species, is there any difference?"

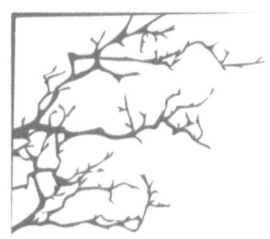

Chapter Five

April grabbed a hairbrush and placed her caramel blonde hair into a ponytail. Her outfit morphed into a short-sleeved, pull-over shirt and three-quarter length pants. Something cool and comfortable for her to drive in, but dressy enough that Robbie wouldn't question their earlier conversation. Her boots transformed into low-heeled sandals that were open at the toes.

"I think it would be best if we don't tell Briella that we are leaving. As I am her Gatherer, she would feel obligated to accompany me. She is so absorbed in her sketching, we should be back before she notices we are gone."

"Yeah, you are right, April."

April retrieved her handbag, opening it for Scout to dive into, then rang Force as she quietly pulled the door closed. "Liam, I am leaving Briella at home while I take a trip to the coast with Scout." April was silent for a minute then said, "Yes, Scout said she will be absorbed in her activities for quite a while." More silence. Scout tried to read April's mind, but she had closed the link. "We should be back before dark. I was just going to check for creatures but Scout informed me the wood nymphs are awakening."

Scout heard Force's swear words loud and clear as April pulled the phone away from her head to protect her eardrum. April was relieved to have gotten far enough to be walking outside the pub, towards her car when his raised voice nearly deafened her. "Sorry, Scout," she mouthed, wishing the fairy hadn't heard.

"I've heard worse," Scout shrugged.

April returned the device to her ear and ended the call. She looked at Scout and said, "He'll be home within the hour. Briella should be fine until then, right?"

"Yes," Scout soothed, putting her friend's mind at ease. "Besides, if she causes any trouble, it should be confined to the room, like the pencil was."

THE HOUSE OF HORRORS

"That's true," April stated opening the door and sitting in the driver's seat. She placed the handbag on the passenger seat. Scout flew for the parcel shelf to retrieve a headset she knew was kept there. She put it on her head after switching it on, and repeated the word, 'breaker,' until April could hear her clearly through the radio speakers.

Scout settled on the dashboard facing the windscreen as April made her way towards the highway.

Calamity and Jacinta were playing on a set of swings in the park with William and Donovan riding past on their horses. The kids gave April a wave as she cruised by.

"Are they supposed to be riding their horses out of the paddock?" Scout asked.

"I don't know," April said glancing at them through the rear-view mirror.

"It's nice to see Jacinta and Calamity getting along."

"Yeah. It's funny how creatures can bring people together sometimes," April said.

"Speaking of together, how are you going to manage the situation when Force is supposed to be your husband and brother-in-law?"

April sighed. She had been wondering the same thing herself but believes she has come up with a partial solution. "I've spoken to Callum, briefly. He has agreed to take on Liam's form, well technically it will be Wade's, for settlement day if he is not hunting a creature. That way the townspeople can see the two of them together.

"After that, I'm not sure how it will work. After all, it is only a holiday home for Wade and me but a permanent residence for Liam so the townspeople would not expect to see the two men together too often. If an occasion arises where they need to be seen together, I will take the form of Wade. I guess we will have to wing it just like the situation with the sensing of creatures in the city while Briella and I are here."

April turned right and travelled another five kilometres before taking the road that would lead to the highway. A few kangaroos were lying in the shade of a tree. "Looks like we are in for another hot, muggy day."

"Do you think we'll get another storm?"

"More than likely."

"Will we be home before then?"

"I don't know," April confessed.

Scout fell silent. She enjoyed the view of the open plain lands, barbed wire fences and scatterings of trees. She loved spotting the odd herd of cows and mob of kangaroos. There were no goats in sight this trip which brought a twang of disappointment. They weren't native to Australia but they sure as heck were funny to watch.

All too soon the landscape changed. They came upon more roads with bitumen tops and houses appeared closer together. Scout could feel the tension increasing in her body. It was an instinctual change in her physiology. Nothing she could control. Scout gritted her teeth and put a smile on her face. Sometimes acting like she was happy made her mood lift enough that she could nearly believe it.

Scout closed her eyes and sent her psyche in search of monster vibes. She was pleased to report the only ones felt at present were of the human variety and not those of their target.

April's stomach growled in hunger causing a giggle to burst from Scout.

"Now how did it know you were nearing a chicken burger restaurant?"

April grinned self-consciously. "It is attached to my eyes, I am sure."

Scout couldn't contain herself. She howled with laughter as another rumble was released. She lay on the dashboard, doubled over, kicking her legs as her arms hugged her abdomen. April looked at her worriedly. "I didn't realise coming to the city was such a big deal for you."

"Yes, it is," Scout said, swallowing down the laughter. "I am glad for the release of tension that your stomach provided."

"But it shouldn't have had that profound an effect on you, Scout," she frowned pulling up to the drive-thru window.

"May I have a large chicken burger meal with cola and a small potato and gravy, please?"

THE HOUSE OF HORRORS

"That will be $10.95." April handed her a twenty dollar note, and was stashing the change when the young man said, "Please drive to the next window." Her order was ready in a couple of minutes. April drove to a rest stop that she frequented often. It had a rectangular pergola with a table and two bench seats made out of wood. Two hundred metres further was a toilet block. There were parking spots for over a dozen cars.

"Why do they have so many carparks if there is only one table provided?"

"There are many situated on this block, Scout. Over that hill, is a sporting field for netball players, but it is busy on that side. I prefer to come around this side, where it is quieter to eat."

"I thought you liked being around people?"

"I do, but I like to eat in peace and quiet. I don't care much for holding a conversation around the dinner table. Once I have eaten, I sometimes walk over the rise and watch the humans play their games. I like to view their interactions. It is interesting."

"Do you miss being human, April?"

"I don't know. It has been so long since I've been one. I think it would be frustrating to not be able to wield the elements. I have learnt to be reliant on my abilities. I do envy their ability to die sometimes."

"Don't you want to live anymore, April?" Scout was growing concerned.

"Yes, I want to live, Scout. Sometimes it is hard outliving everybody. Every friend that is human will die. You can't be friends with them for long because they start to wonder why they look older but you don't."

"It sounds like you need to fall in love with a Gatherer. That way you would never be lonely."

"That didn't work out so well for Rochelle now, did it?"

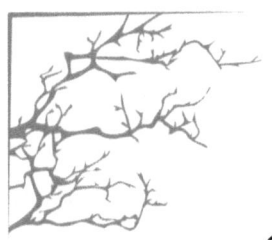

Chapter Six

Scout went quiet. She hadn't meant to bring up memories of Rochelle and Toren's broken love-affair so soon. Just as she had cautioned Briella earlier with her sketch, she should've taken stock of the words that were coming out of her own mouth before she said them. "I'm sorry, April. I didn't mean to remind you that Sarina turned Toren into a vampire and took him back to Mystique."

April touched Scout gently on the shoulder. "Toren and Rochelle are never far from my thoughts," she replied. "Are we going to eat or what?"

'What!' Scout thought keeping the word to herself. She didn't eat food prepared by humans. Scout survived on mushrooms and the odd berry, with nectar supplying her liquid requirements. She fluttered out of the car rather than hitching a ride.

There weren't any people in the near vicinity. April brought her bag with her just in case Scout needed to hide quickly.

Once April had spread her food across the table, she reached into her bag and unzipped a secret compartment. Inside was Scout's favourite mushroom, the one with the dusky pink flesh and a couple of mulberries for dessert. Scout eyed them suspiciously. "When did you pack those?"

"This morning, after we finished cleaning off the pencil from the walls."

"Who were you planning on bringing with you?"

"You," April admitted with a smirk as she added some chips to her burger before taking a bite.

"You were that sure I would come with you?"

April looked at her long and hard. "You are a fantastic friend to Briella, Scout. I knew you would put your discomfort over being near the beach aside if you thought you were helping your friend. A point you confirmed earlier when we were discussing the need for you to move into the apartment when we want a short holiday. I am sorry, though, and feel I need to offer you a huge apology. I didn't realise how strongly the adverse effects of being here were for you."

Scout knew April wouldn't purposely put her in an uncomfortable position. "I also know how seriously you take your job; detecting, locating and tracking non-indigenous creatures that are harmful to humans. You wouldn't allow the area to go unprotected any longer once you knew it had not been surveyed for more than a week. Your conscience wouldn't allow it. I just figured it would be easier to spring it on you than to give you advanced warning. I thought it might help with your anxiety levels, but I can see I was wrong to think that."

"It doesn't matter, April. As you said, I would have come anyway, and I won't let my afflictions get in the way of doing a great job. How does Briella manage to combat this trouble with her magic every year?"

"I didn't even know she had issues during Halloween. She has somehow kept it hidden from me. I don't know who, if anybody, has been helping to keep it contained."

"We'll have to ask her. Later, when things have gone back to normal."

"Yeah. I guess she does the same as you. Realise there is an issue but not let it rule her life. Now that I think about it, city people are more likely to not dwell on things, and there is a higher tolerance for weird or different than I imagine there would be in smaller, country towns.

"Maybe," Scout reluctantly agreed. She didn't really have anything to gauge April's words against. For most of her life, Scout had done everything she could to avoid humans.

They ate the rest of their meal in silence. April offered Scout some of her thickshake. When Scout declined a taste, April brought out a pink daisy blossom. "My favourite!" Scout exclaimed.

"I know," April smirked, "Briella told me."

April threw her containers in the rubbish bin and walked back to the car with Scout on her shoulder. "Would you like to see our apartment before we drive to the hinterlands?"

"Sure," Scout answered with excitement. She had been curious to see where Briella had lived for the past few decades.

"How have you stayed here so long without people asking questions about your age and stuff?"

Scout couldn't read the expression on April's face. It was a look that had never been presented to her by Force before. "You'll see," she answered simply.

Scout's psyche became more agitated the closer they came to the city centre. She thought that once they drove through to the other side, the buildings would thin out. She was wrong. They doubled in number and towered over the buildings they had passed earlier.

"Do you live in one of these?" Scout asked with huge eyes.

"Yep."

"How do you stand it?"

"This is how I get to stay in one place. Most of these units are investment properties. The owners rent them out to holidaymakers. There is only one other family who lives here permanently, and once

45

the children grow up, they won't take any notice of me anymore. By then, I will be sporting an older hairstyle, and the memory of me will fade into the background."

"How can you say that, April? You are gorgeous. Nobody is going to forget a face like yours."

"Sure they do, Scout. I don't talk to them much. In fact, I make sure to discourage a friendship with the permanent residents. That way, they see me as a young beach going holidaymaker myself. I am hardly ever out and about when they are coming and going, so they forget I live here and just assume I am another blonde surfer chick or sunbather in a swimsuit and towel."

"Lucky you have the battle suit. It can help you set up any scene you want to portray."

"Exactly," April replied as her button-up shirt became a one-piece swimsuit and her three-quarter pants became a wetsuit. "Are you ready?" April parked the car and waited for a response.

"Sure," Scout lied, climbing inside the handbag.

An elevator took them to the top floor and opened onto a room that had floor-to-ceiling windows. Scout flew around the room impressed by the view. "You have an ocean view on two sides. Your building is the tallest of them all. How can you afford this, April?"

"I own this building, Scout."

"You do?"

"Yes. When you have lived as long as I have you learn a thing or two. As long as I don't become complacent, and keep abreast of changes, I am able to continue increasing my wealth."

"Is Force wealthy like you?"

April opened her mouth but stopped herself from speaking until she had thought about what she was going to say. "That is a conversation best left between the two of you."

Scout couldn't resent April for her answer. It actually made her like April even more to know that she wouldn't discuss his personal stuff with others, not even her. Just to be sure, though, she flew to a white leather single seater and perched on the back. "Do you think there is anything between Force and Loretta?

April glanced over at Scout then turned towards a door to the left that Scout hadn't noticed. "They are friends, aren't they?" she answered stepping into the room and closing the door. Scout wondered what she was doing then heard the flush of a toilet.

As soon as she appeared again, Scout continued her line of questioning. "Do you think he loves her?"

April stared at Scout not knowing whether to laugh or cringe. Was the fairy testing her? A closer look revealed something April hadn't considered. "Scout, do you have feelings for Liam?"

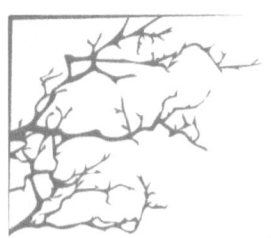

Chapter Seven

"Of course, I do. I care about all of the Gatherers I work with. You know what I mean?"

Scout placed a look of innocence on her face, but April wasn't buying it. She took a couple of pieces of underwear from a basket lying in the corner of the living room and placed them in her handbag. "I suppose you expect me to sit on those on the way down?"

"They're clean," April answered a tad defensively. "And stop changing the subject. Do you care about Force more than the others?"

"Of course I do. I work more closely with him and know him better than you or any of the others."

April sighed, as she sat on the nearest chair. "Does he know you love him?"

"Don't be ridiculous. I am a fairy. He is a Gatherer for Pete's sake!"

April moved towards her. Scout panicked and fluttered backwards. She glanced around for somewhere to hide. She didn't want to deal with any more questions. Her eyes landed on the coffee table that had been pushed over near the wall. Perched on top was Briella's beautiful home. Scout gasped with delight.

April wanted to continue the conversation but knew no good would come from it. Scout was obviously in denial and Force was no doubt unaware of her affections. If April didn't back off, Scout would probably not come to her when realisation set in. Perhaps, she wouldn't choose to discuss the matter with April when the time came, anyway. April wasn't sure she would broach the subject with Briella either, with the two of them being so close. She decided to give Scout some breathing room.

"It's unlocked if you want to go inside."

"Do you think Briella would mind?"

THE HOUSE OF HORRORS

"No, she won't mind. I wouldn't go inviting the neighbourhood fairies for a party in her absence, though."

Scout chuckled quietly as she took a closer look at the design. The house was white with a dark grey shingled roof and trimmings. The front veranda was elegant in appearance with supporting columns similar to those found in a Hercules movie. The windows that weren't covered with curtains showed potted plants leaning against the glass from the inside.

Scout turned the knob on the door and pushed it open. April called after her, "You've got ten minutes, Scout."

"Okay." Scout's voice was lost in the spaciousness inside. She was exposed to an open-plan design. Wallpaper of a tropical forest was stuck to the walls of the living and dining areas. The kitchen walls were decorated with a pale green tile. Wood-grained linoleum seemed to be the flooring of choice. An option far easier to maintain than the real thing.

Scout moved further into the house and found a study that was lined with bookshelves from floor to ceiling on three sides of the room. On the fourth wall was the door that Scout had entered through and a log fireplace. Scout moved a grill to the side to see if a chimney linked the fireplace to the outside. It appeared as though it did.

Off the study was a bedroom that was painted in a pale blue. It had a built-in-wardrobe which contained two cabinets of hanging space, a three drawer system for delicates and five shelves for folded clothes to sit on, all of which were empty. A double bed sat in the middle of the far wall and was covered with a bedspread that had pictures of Orcas, stingrays and fish. There was a three drawer cupboard located on each side of the bed that was made from teak wood.

Scout backtracked and found herself in a games room. There was table tennis set up for one, a billiards table, a basketball hoop attached to a wall and a hopscotch grid painted on the floor. Walking into the next room brought her exploration to a halt.

THE HOUSE OF HORRORS

Scout's face lit up with wonder as she surveyed the mini-putt-putt golf course that spanned three rooms.

A quick perusal of the ceiling failed to show how the length of this area was possible. April had used wider beams in this section of the house to provide support for the weight of the roof, but these were hidden by the ceiling.

Scout picked up a putter with a lilac grip from the cabinet and gently swung the club. Perfect height and weight. She grabbed an orange golf ball and began to play.

The first hole took four strokes to sink the ball. "Are you kidding me?" Scout muttered, plucking the ball from the cup and lining it up on the next green. This time she sank it in two shots. "Now, that's more like it," she grinned, setting up for the next. She pulled the club back smoothly then brought it forward right when April called her name.

The club picked up speed as she jumped like a child who had been caught doing something wrong. The putter head hit the ball a bit harder than she had planned and it shot across the fake grass at high speed. "Oh no," she cried, swiftly spreading her wings in anticipation of a disaster. The roof came up, and April reached down her hand, stopping the ball from putting a dent in the wall.

"I thought you were having a look through Briella's house."

"I was, am. I am," Scout replied. "Well, I was until I found this room. April, this is amazing. Does Briella play in here often?"

"I don't know. You'll have to ask her."

"How much time does she spend in her home?"

"Not a lot. Most of the time she is with me. Speaking of Briella, we should get going. The sooner we get to the hinterlands to see if Wynomiah is awake, the sooner we can get back and check on her."

April waited for Scout to fly out before closing the roof. She then made her way to the kitchen and took a couple of bottles of cola from the fridge and a couple of bottles of water. She placed them in a cooler bag with an ice brick.

Scout fluttered to April's handbag and nestled herself inside, as far away from April's underwear as she could manage. As soon as April lifted the bag, the cup of a bra fell on top of her. "Dammit!" Scout cursed.

"Be grateful I'm not a D cup or bigger," April's voice was muffled by the material. Scout threw the item aside in a huff. April laughed, "You're just jealous."

Scout looked at her own chest and decided she had nothing to be jealous about.

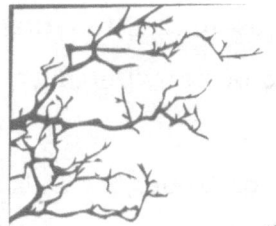

Chapter Eight

It was wonderful to be back in her hinterlands, but Scout realised it was no nicer in these woods than her new location. The trees were just as magnificent, the shadows just as mysterious and the sound of animals splashing through water just as glorious to her spirit.

April breathed in the air with a grimace. To her, the forest smelled of dank moss, rotting vegetation and mould. Scout sat on April's shoulder as she meandered along the natural pathways. The layout had changed slightly since she had visited last and it took a few moments for her to get her bearings and choose the correct path to their destination.

"Do you think she will talk to us?" Scout asked, fluttering her wings slightly.

"I don't know, Scout. I'm not sure she still resides here."

"What makes you think she might have moved?"

"Wood nymphs don't leave their forest, Scout. They become one with a tree for the rest of that tree's existence. Once the tree dies, so too, does the wood nymph."

"But that is terrible," Scout lowered her head as a sign of respect for those who had fallen.

"Do you think the tree has died?"

"I'm not sure. My nature vibes are vibrating. I think a natural disaster has hit this part of the forest recently."

"When you say recently, how long ago are we talking?"

"Anywhere up to fifty years."

"Right," Scout cried as April suddenly stopped, and she nearly toppled forwards. "Careful!"

"Sorry." April surveyed their surroundings then closed her eyes. Without opening them, she squatted and placed her fingertips on the ground in front of her. Scout had seen Force do this before, and knew April was conversing with nature. "I'm pretty sure this is the tree," she told Scout.

April stood and contemplated the twisted limbs before her. With a gentle touch, she placed her palm on the scratchy bark and called to the wood nymph. As she expected, there was no answer. A further five attempts to make contact with Wynomiah went unanswered. "I guess she is gone."

"Seems like it," Scout agreed, gently stroking the skin on April's neck. "Did you want to check other areas in case we are standing in the wrong spot?

"No. I am pretty sure this was Wynomiah's tree."

"But the tree is still alive. Wouldn't that mean that Wynomiah is, too?"

"Yes, she would still be alive, but because of the extent of damage to the tree, it will take her a long time to heal herself, and she will not be aware of what is going on around her while that process is taking place. I probably should have used the term 'inaccessible' instead of 'gone'. I guess we will not be able to confirm Dynopiah's claim."

"You said yourself, her predictions explain a lot with the increase in monster attacks."

THE HOUSE OF HORRORS

"Monsters! Really, Scout. Don't let Queen Adair or the Guardians hear you calling the creatures, monsters."

"Yeah, I know. But they are monsters, April. No doubt about it."

"That may be the case, but you know the queen's stance on having them viewed in a negative light."

"They should be regarded that way. They hurt people," Scout interrupted.

"For their own survival, Scout. Never forget that. What wouldn't you do to stay alive?"

"I wouldn't hurt people," she mumbled.

"Are you sure about that? If it was them, or you . . . "

Scout fell silent. She would like to think she wouldn't injure another creature to stay alive, but she wasn't sure. When it really came down to it, would she have the courage to do whatever it took to survive? She hoped she would never have to find out. They wandered out of the forest together and made their way to the car. The trip home was uncomfortable for Scout. She sat on the back seat with her headset, hiding from the brightness of the sun streaming through the windscreen.

"I'll look into getting you some sunglasses, Scout. I'll pull up some websites on the Internet when we get back, and you can choose a couple of styles that you like. They will take a few days to arrive, but when they do, and you shrink them down, you won't have any more issues with the sunlight hurting your eyes.

"April, I fly around in the sun all the time."

"Do you really? From what Force tells me, you generally fly at night."

"Unless I am hunting a monster, at which time I fly whenever is necessary. My eyes are fine when I am flying in the open. It is only in the car that my eyes hurt when the beams of light are being magnified by the glass."

"Think how cool you will look," April's smile came through the tone of her voice.

"What? You don't think I am already?"

"Sure, I do, Scout. With a pair of sunglasses and a black shirt instead of that purple one, you could be mistaken for one of the men in black."

THE HOUSE OF HORRORS

"You mean woman in black," Scout stated, never having heard of the 'Men in Black' story franchise.

April appreciated how close she and Briella were at that moment. The fashion tips they shared, the stories they read together, the movies they watched. Their lives were so intertwined with one another, they were almost as close as twins. Such a pity that Scout didn't have that sort of relationship with somebody. She was close to Force, for sure, but they didn't live for one another like she and Briella did. April could only hope that their jobs willing, Briella and Scout would get to spend a lot more time together. April wanted Scout to feel as though she was part of a family.

Her thoughts drifted to the pumpkins in the pumpkin patch. Even as close as they were, Briella had kept a secret from her for centuries. She didn't know whether to feel upset or angry about that. Would she have told Scout, if they hadn't discovered her secret on their own? April knew that was a question she would never know the answer to.

The first thing they did when they entered the pub was run up the stairs, Scout nestled safely inside the handbag once more, to check on Briella. When they came into the room, it felt empty.

"Briella?" April called as Scout fluttered over to the art studio.

"She's not here," Scout confirmed. Glancing around the room, they were unable to locate any clues as to her whereabouts. Scout shivered as a coldness seeped into the room.

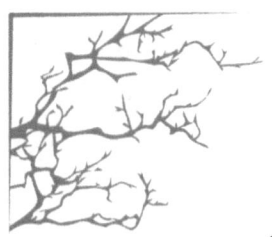

Chapter Nine

April and Scout rushed to Force's room but still no Briella. By this time, April was in a panic. She opened her mind-link to connect to Briella as the door to the bathroom opened. Force stood in the doorway with a towel wrapped around his waist, a huge welcoming smile on his face. He opened his mouth to say hello when April flew into a rage. "You locked Briella in the mushroom cupboard?"

"Settle, April," he raised his hand defensively as she advanced towards him. "She is perfectly safe and hasn't been there for more than a few minutes."

"That is not what she is telling me," April fisted her hands and prepared to strike, as Scout released Briella from the cupboard.

"Now, now. You know physical violence never solved anything."

"You're right," she smiled, opening her hands to reveal a blue coloured fireball in each palm.

"That is going to cost us our deposit on the rooms," he reminded her.

"I don't care." She drew her right hand back and felt a feather-like touch across her wrist. She glanced down at her hand to see Briella and Scout wrapped around her arm. "Out of the way, girls," April warned.

"Don't hurt him, April," Scout shouted, huffing and puffing with effort.

'I'm fine. I might have exaggerated the situation a little,' Briella confessed. "Or a lot," she added quietly.

April snuffed out the flames and scolded Briella. "You shouldn't put me in a position where I will defend you unnecessarily, Briella. You know what Liam and I are capable of, and things could very quickly get out of hand."

Briella wasn't going to be lectured by April. "You shouldn't resort to battle tactics whenever your anger is brought to the surface. Geez, April. You should have learnt how to control your temper by now."

"Excuse me?" April's face was flushed, and her eyes were cold as ice. "Briella, when I found you missing from our room and there was no sign of you in here, I was terrified for you." Force stepped forward cautiously and placed his right arm on her shoulder. When April didn't push him away, he pulled her towards him and wrapped her in his arms.

"Come on, April. Let it go. You know how incorrigible the fairies can be. I brought Briella in here because she had been sketching for hours and needed a break. She was getting stroppy from lack of food so I put her in the mushroom cupboard to encourage her to eat while I had my shower. I'm sorry I never thought to write you a note to let you know she was here with me. Why don't you go have a shower, and I'll take you out for dinner?" April pushed back and looked into his eyes. They were the colour of milk chocolate.

"Liam, your eyes?"

He answered her in a private mind-link. '*I know you all think I can't remember to change my eye colour to a natural human colour. I can. I choose not to.'* Using his mouth to speak he said, "Come to dinner with me, April."

"I would like that," she answered. "But you're not wearing that."

He looked down at himself and said, "Why not? What's wrong with what I'm wearing?" His grin was infectious, and April felt her anger melt away. "Who's incorrigible?" she asked.

"I'm going! Wear something comfortable," he said as he stepped into the bedroom, a space behind a partition.

"What do you consider to be comfortable clothing?"

"Your battle suit. It can morph into whatever the other patrons are wearing."

"Where are we going?"

"To a lovely little place down the road."

April was becoming frustrated. Why did he talk in riddles when she needed him to tell it straight? "What's the name of the place?"

"The Devil's Gate."

"I'm not fighting it out with demons, Liam. I've had a long day. Oh no. I forgot. Robbie is cooking me a steak for dinner."

"No, he's not. I've cancelled your booking."

"You did what?"

"He's cooked you dinner eighty percent of the time you've been here, and I want to take you out. I think he fancies you."

"Don't be ridiculous. He's old enough to be my grandfather."

"Now who's being ridiculous?" he stated, walking into the living area in blue jeans, plaid shirt and cowboy boots.

"Where's your hat?"

"Don't change the subject. Robbie could have been your great, great, great, great . . ."

"Oh stop it," she laughed, plucking a cushion from the lounge chair and throwing it at him.

"Great, great, great, great, grandson. Don't be long. We're leaving in twenty minutes."

"That's not enough time to get ready," she squealed, racing for the door.

"Of course it is. Three minutes in the shower, two to get dry and fifteen minutes to decide which battle suit you are going to wear. Here's a hint. They are identical to one another, so it doesn't matter."

"OOOOOH!" Her voice could still be heard through the door she had slammed shut.

"Wow, Force. You know how to get a lady riled up." Scout flew up to his face and gave the finger he extended a high-five.

"You girls be good while we are gone. No getting up to mischief, okay?"

"Okay," they cried in unison.

Force walked to the bathroom to clean his teeth. Briella raised an eyebrow. "Shouldn't he have done that before he got dressed? What if he spills toothpaste all over himself?"

"His battle suit will remove it. Doesn't April ever spill anything on her clothes?"

"No. She is the daintiest eater I've ever seen. She can wolf down a burger in seconds, yet it is done elegantly. Have you never taken any notice?"

THE HOUSE OF HORRORS

"Can't say that I have," Scout shrugged her shoulders. "So, have you finished the picture of the house, or do you still have more sketching to do?"

"I'm finished, unless you want to make some adjustments. Come and take a look."

Neither Force's door nor April's was locked so the fairies had no problem gaining entry to April's room. They headed straight to the art studio. Flying over the wall rather than using the doorway. Briella indicated the chair to Scout then waited for her to be seated.

"I have worked really hard on this, which I am sure you will realise once you see the detail in the sketch. What you can't see or appreciate is the detail I have put into the rooms that are hidden beneath the top layer. It might look a bit strange at first, but once you sprinkle some magic over the page and bring it to life, I am sure you will be as impressed with my effort as I am."

"Will you just show me the damned picture?" Briella reached in front of Scout and flipped the cover of her sketchbook up. Scout's eyes widened, and a small gasp escaped her lips. She leaned forward and gently rubbed her finger across the picture. "Briella, this is your best work yet."

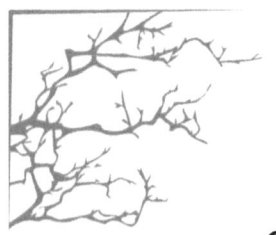

Chapter Ten

The picture was a mess with Briella having drawn layer upon layer. It was a bit hard to imagine what it would look like when it was converted to 3D. So why did Scout tell her it was fantastic?

She could tell from the vibe the paper gave off when she touched it. A shiver ran along her finger, through the palm of her hand, up her arm and into her spine. A sure sign that something wonderful was about to occur.

"We need to find somewhere out of the way to set it up so we can go inside and explore."

"Why don't we just pop it out onto the floor behind the lounge suite in Force's room? Liam and April will be out for a few hours, so we'll have some time to check it out and convert it to 2D before they get back."

"I have a feeling April is not going to like where Force is taking her. I doubt we will have an hour let alone two."

"Well, there's no room here. April has bits of house stashed all over the place under cover so I can't take a peek."

"Then we'll have to find somewhere outside."

"Oh, how exciting," Briella rubbed her hands together. "We'll have to bring lanterns with us so we can see our way around in the dark. You've got some in your room, haven't you? It will be as spooky as bats in a belfry."

"When have you ever seen bats in a belfry in your lifetime?"

"Never, but I can just imagine how scary that would be," Briella shivered.

"Fine, but we'll have to wait for Force and April to leave before we head outside."

"Head outside to do what?" Force sprang on them, as he entered April's room.

"I wish you wouldn't sneak up on us like that," Scout admonished him.

"If you weren't trying to sneak around all the time, you wouldn't be so jumpy. What are you two up to?"

"Nothing," Scout said.

"None of your business!" Briella shouted defiantly.

"Hmmm, you need to work on that, Briella. Definitely up to something. Come on, spit it out."

"It's a surprise for Halloween," Scout said before Briella could open her mouth.

"For whom?"

"April and yourself," Briella jutted her chin and raised her head slightly.

"Well, all right then. Make sure you stay together and keep an eye out for danger." 'What am I saying?' he thought. 'I know what you two are like when you're up to something.' Speaking to them he said, "Here, take this."

Scout and Briella looked at the item in his hand. It was a tiny aerosol can. Mind you, it was humongous to them. "What is it?" Scout asked.

"Pepper spray."

"What do we want that for?"

73

"You don't. Briella does. She can't use her magic at the moment, but she needs something to protect herself with. If you are in trouble with a live predator, spray this in their eyes or mouth, and you should be able to get away safely."

"Hmmm," Briella scrunched up her mouth as she flew towards the object. "It's a bit big, don't you think?"

"Scout can shrink it for you."

"Won't be much use then, will it?"

Force frowned as his finger tapped his chin. "It is still better than nothing."

"I doubt it," she said but took it anyway. Briella thought she would be safer using her magic and suffering the consequences. Perhaps if her magic made inanimate objects come to life, it would make animated creatures go into some sort of stasis until sunrise. She didn't particularly want to test that theory, but if her life was at stake, she would have no qualms whatsoever.

"What time do you think you'll be home?" Scout asked him.

"The place closes at ten."

THE HOUSE OF HORRORS

"Where is the Devil's Gate?" Briella queried.

"In the city."

"How come I've never heard of it?"

"It's out of bounds for fairies."

"What sort of establishment is out of bounds for fairies?" Scout wrinkled up her nose.

"The sort that doesn't concern you," he snickered.

"What kind of place are you taking her to?" Scout demanded, thinking it was somewhere seedy.

Force opened a mind-link between him and Scout only. *'It is kind of like a circus-themed restaurant that has fire twirlers and contortionists for entertainment.'*

'Oh, yeah. April will love that,' Scout replied with a smile.

Briella looked from one to the other. "You are talking without me, aren't you?" she stamped her foot while pouting.

"I'll just knock on the bathroom door to hurry April up. She's had her twenty minutes."

"Are you serious? She's already exploded at you once today!"

"Yeah right," he laughed, imagining her anger meter rising. "Should I take a shield with me?"

"Absolutely," Briella giggled. "It had better be made out of the same stuff Captain America's is made from."

"Pfft. Mine is way better than his."

The fairies howled with laughter. "Men. Always got to be better, bigger, smarter than the next guy." Scout stated.

"I heard that," Force said.

"Have you got your keys?" Scout asked.

"Yep," he replied.

"Wallet?"

"Crap, no." He collected his jacket and keys from the kitchen and headed out the door.

A couple of minutes later, April appeared out of the bathroom, looking lovely in her battle suit, her caramel hair loose on her shoulders. She began to get annoyed again when she saw that Force was not waiting for her. Briella read the signs and jumped in before April's anger escalated.

"Force forgot his wallet and went back to his room to get it. If you go now, you should meet him at his door."

Opening the door with a smile, April said, "Thanks girls. See you later. Be good, now."

"Geez, I thought they'd never leave," Briella brightened with enthusiasm. "I'll get the sketchbook and we'll go to Force's room where we can grab some mushrooms, a couple of drinks, and the lanterns. Ooh, this is going to be so good. I can't wait to see my creation as I've pictured it in my head."

"Yeah, it's going to be awesome," Scout replied.

Briella tried to open the door but it was locked up tight. "Scout, can you get the door, please?"

Scout flew over, and with a little fairy dust, they were out of April's room and headed for Force's. Scout gained them entry, allowing Briella to collect the lanterns from a bench along the living room wall. "These are perfect," she said, admiring the star patterns in the metal work that would showcase Scout's fairy dust housed inside.

Scout grabbed a couple of clear bottles containing a swirling pink liquid to go with the mushrooms and mulberries and placed them in her satchel.

"Are you ready?" Briella fluttered into the kitchenette.

"Absolutely."

Like the day before, they exited through a window rather than navigate the inside of the pub where they might be seen. The strap of Scout's satchel sat securely over her shoulder and a lantern dangled from her hand. Briella held her lantern and the sketchpad. "So where are we going?"

"There's a streetlight at the end of the carpark. If we place the paper there and you sprinkle your magic, we should be able to get a good look at the exterior of the house before we enter. It will help to set the mood," Briella said.

"What if someone sees it?"

"There's an industrial bin right beside the entry. If we set it up on the other side, no-one coming in will be able to spot it. We should be finished with our inspection before anyone is ready to leave. The house will be back in its 2D form and tucked away safely in our art studio."

By the time they had finished their discussion, they had arrived at their destination. Scout could hardly contain her excitement as Briella laid the sketchpad on the gravel. "Whenever you're ready," she grinned.

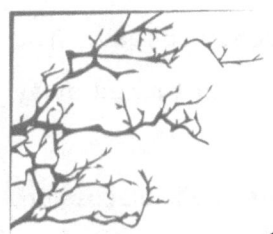

Chapter Eleven

Briella whooped with delight as her house came off the page and went through the assembly process. Scout took a few steps back as the dilapidated structure came to life. The roof appeared to be in perfect condition. It seemed to be constructed of dark grey shingles, the pitch as high as a tower.

The building was two storeys high. There were two bay windows on the bottom level, one to the left of a narrow veranda and the other to the right of the front door. Directly above was another bay window that jutted onto the roof and a conical towered roof above that.

There wasn't one intact window in the place. The openings were either covered in broken glass or shuttered up with tacked on boards. The unpainted wood was a deep brown. When Briella looked at

Scout, her eyes glowed with happiness. "It's just like I imagined."

"Well you did say it would scare my pants off, and I've got to say, they are hanging on by a thread."

"Let's go inside," Briella reached for Scout's arm.

Scout pulled out of reach. "Are you kidding?"

Briella's face fell a little. "Come on, Scout. I spent hours drawing this. The least you can do is have a look inside."

Scout looked like she didn't think that was a good idea. "I know, Briella, it just looks so scary."

"That's the whole point. It's a prop for Halloween. If it were all fairy tale castles and stuff, it would look out of place. It won't hurt you. I haven't created any rooms where spikes come out of the walls or trapdoors send you into a pit of despair. Everything inside is safe, I promise."

"How do we get in? Is the broken glass sharp, or is it just for show?"

"I'm not sure. I've never drawn anything like this before."

A burst of laughter had them freezing like statues. They listened nervously to the voices getting closer. They couldn't tell if it was two women approaching or two pubescent boys.

"What do we do?"

"Get in the house."

"Are you kidding? What if they see it?"

"Better they see the house than the two of us."

Scout rocked her head from side to side as she weighed up their options. After a few seconds, she realised they didn't have any. Scout followed Briella's lead, pleased to see that the door was capable of opening and closing. It was dark inside, and once Briella closed the door, Scout couldn't see the hand she'd raised in front of her face. Her finger began to glow as she readied herself to release some fairy dust into the lantern.

"Wait," Briella cautioned.

"What for?"

"The people to leave the area."

"Why? They won't be able to see it from the outside."

"What if they can? Please wait, Scout."

THE HOUSE OF HORRORS

"Fine, but I can't see a damned thing." She shrieked when Briella's hand landed on her upper arm.

"It's just me. Man, jumpy much."

"Sorry," Scout whispered as the voices drew closer. Scout and Briella huddled together and held their breath. When they were nearly out of air, Scout sucked in a lungful, frightening them both. A smack to the arm from Briella and a 'don't do that,' later, they realised the voices were moving away.

"Do you think it's safe to light the lanterns?"

"Yeah, I reckon it is," Briella stated confidently.

Scout's finger glowed, and a stream of golden fairy dust flew from the tip of her finger and into a star on one of the sides. It swirled around, igniting the special fairy gas that floated inside. Scout felt a lot better now that she could see. She quickly set about lighting Briella's lamp to prevent her from using magic, then took the time to look around the room.

They were standing in an entryway. Directly ahead was a staircase to the upper level and a parallel hallway to the right. There wasn't any furniture in this part of the house, just straight clean lines. As a result, although the walls weren't coloured and appeared to be the same dark brown colour as the outside walls, the house felt open and welcoming. "Where should we go first?" Scout inquired, warming up to the place.

"Wherever your heart desires," Briella answered.

"Why don't we start on the ground level and work our way up?" she suggested.

"Good idea," Briella concurred.

Briella allowed Scout to lead the way. She hadn't asked for a tour, so Briella let Scout discover things at her own pace. To the right was a formal lounge room, with three black leather lounges that each seated two, a coffee table in the middle and an upright piano along the far wall.

Further along was a formal dining room with a rectangular table that seated twelve. A chandelier, which appeared to be made out of clear crystals, hung from the ceiling in the middle of the room. At the back of the house was the kitchen with an abundance of cabinets up high and down low on every wall.

THE HOUSE OF HORRORS

In the middle was a dining room table that was square and had four wooden chairs, one on each side. Past that was a deck that served as an entertaining area.

To the left of the entry was a guest bedroom with a double bed in the middle of the far wall and two bedside tables. Two lanterns hung on the wall above the cabinets. A walk-in-robe and ensuite were attached to the room by a private door. A study, with a desk that held a lamp and globe of the world on its surface, a couple of chairs, and some bookcases, was next along the hallway. The last room on the lower level was the entertainment room with widescreen television, wireless speaker system and reclining chairs in floral tapestry print.

Scout glanced at Briella. "This is pretty amazing. You should have designed our house."

"Oh, no. I couldn't do that. Wait until you see April's masterpiece. It will put my creation to shame."

"I doubt it," Scout said as she headed for the stairs. "What's up there?"

"Go on up and have a look," she smiled, not wanting to give anything away.

Scout was pretty sure she knew what was up there. More bedrooms, bathrooms, and wardrobes. Boy, was she mistaken!

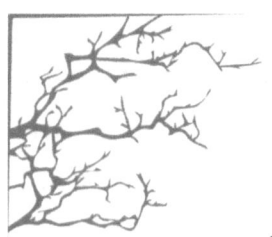

Chapter Twelve

It was literally a house of horrors. There was only one room. There were no walls, architraves, or doorways to separate the space. No concertinaed dividers or wardrobe sized furniture to divide the area either.

What it did have was a torture rack in the middle of the room, chains attached to the wall and a bed of nails along the far wall. A pillory was placed at the top of the stairs ready to imprison somebody inside. A casket leaned against the wall to the right. A figure of a werewolf was prepared to pounce on the left. "What's in the coffin, Briella?"

"What do you think might be in there?"

"A vampire?"

"That would be correct."

"How life-like is it?"

"As real looking as everything else in this room."

"I think I'd like to leave now."

"Okay," Briella frowned, turning around to walk down the stairs. "Are you sure you don't want a closer look at my treasures? There is a lot more to see."

"Yes, I'm sure. They are very well drawn. I am in awe of your sketching ability."

"But you don't want a close-up?"

"I don't do horror very well. It's all a bit too life-like for me."

"Fair enough. I'll take that as a compliment," she said, finally descending the staircase. Scout was close on her heels.

"You probably think I am a wuss."

"Not at all," Briella smirked, thinking that exactly. "Each to their own."

The fairies suddenly lost their footing and slammed against the wall before being flung against the handrail.

"Scout!"

"Briella!" They cried out simultaneously. "What's happening?"

"I don't know," Briella shrieked.

"Did you get your fairy dust on anything?"

"Nope, no leakages from moi."

They tumbled to the bottom of the stairs and lay in a tangled heap. That was when they heard the voices from earlier.

"This will make a wonderful Christmas gift for Justine, once we've fixed it up," voice one said.

"Are you sure it doesn't belong to somebody?" the same voice answered.

"It belongs to us. If we don't take it, Russell will put it in his pick-up in the morning and throw it in his fire pit. He hasn't done a good burning in a while, so I bet it is full of all sorts of rubbish just waiting to be cremated."

"It would be a shame to see this old thing go up in flames. Apart from the windows, the structure of the rest of the dollhouse looks pretty sound. Makes you wonder why anybody would throw it away, don't you think?"

"Absolutely."

Scout and Briella flew over to the windows and peered through the holes in the glass. It was too dark to see who had hold of them. "Scout, what are we going to do?"

"Well, we are not going to panic. We'll have to make a fly for it. Then we can follow them and find out where they are taking it. Force or April can collect it in the morning as stolen property."

"Great idea. Who's going first?"

"I will. Stay right behind me. On three; one, two, three." Scout ran for the door and flung it open. She dropped the lantern on the floor and then flew through the doorway. The boy holding the house suddenly began swatting at her yelling, "William, the blasted mozzies are buzzing around. Don't let them bite you. You know how allergic we are."

"Leave the house here. We'll come back for it in the morning."

"No, I can't do that!" he yelled, swinging around in circles. "Somebody might pinch it, or damage it beyond repair."

"Then we'll get Justine another present."

"This would make a cool Halloween gift, you know."

THE HOUSE OF HORRORS

"Yeah, but Christmas celebrations go on for weeks, whereas Halloween is just a couple of days."

"Yeah, you're right. How are we going to strap the house to your bike, William?"

"We can't, Donovan. You run with the house, and I'll take care of the bikes."

"Mum and Dad are going to be annoyed when we get home late."

"They won't be when they see the reason why. Besides they are used to us getting into mischief. They should have thought more seriously about sending us on their errands."

"That's right."

Scout breathed a sigh of relief. At least she knew who they were now. The twins helped Force release the kids who had been captured by the Jealousy Monsters. Force cured Donovan of Leukaemia once he discovered the boy had the condition and ensured that his brother would never develop the disease. If nothing else, the boys owed them. So if worse came to worst, Scout would make sure to remind them of that fact. Of course, they had no memory of her. That had been wiped by April.

91

Scout managed to get out of the danger zone between Donovan and the house. She flew behind them making sure to remain in the shadows. She wasn't too concerned about losing sight of them. She knew where they lived. Her concern was that Briella wasn't behind her. Was she stuck in the house?

Briella was lying unconscious on the floor, fairy dust seeping from her pores. She had a few bruises from being thrown against the walls as Donovan shook the house. The dust seeped into the floorboards and quickly spread throughout the house. The house began to glow a vibrant golden colour, frightening Donovan to the point where he set it on the ground. "What the hell?" he stared at the house that seemed to shimmer before his eyes.

"Did you see that?" William asked, rubbing his eyes with his fists.

"It was like the house yawned," Donovan squeaked timidly.

"I think it's time to leave," William said.

THE HOUSE OF HORRORS

"I concur," Donovan replied. He reached for the handlebars of his bike when the house grew to the size of an average two-story house.

"Da, Da, Da," William stuttered with fright.

Donovan opened and closed his mouth a few times before being sucked into the building. His screams were cut off as his brother was pulled in after him and collided with his back, knocking him to the ground, and winding him.

William climbed off his brother and shook him, "Donovan, Donovan, don't die on me."

"I'm not going to die," he wheezed painfully. "Stop shaking me," he implored, trying to get a decently sized breath into his lungs.

"Thank the Lord, you are still with me."

"William, I think we should have left those mushrooms alone."

"Yeah, me too." A thud upstairs had the boys tilting their heads. "It's just a dream," William muttered to himself.

Donovan doubted it was possible for twins to experience the same dream. "Get up."

"I'm not going up there."

"Who said anything about going upstairs? I'm headed for the front door, but you can continue to lie there if you like."

William scrambled to his feet and followed closely behind his brother. Donovan reached for the handle and pulled as hard as he could. The door refused to budge. "It must have locked itself. Look around for a key."

William looked behind him. There was not a piece of furniture in sight. He glanced back at Donovan who was searching the frame of the door for a hook that might hold the key. William moved to the window to see if they could exit that way. When he placed his hand against the glass, he was thrown across the room as though being hit with a surge of electricity.

Donovan swore as he raced to help his brother. He gazed into William's eyes and felt a tad relieved to see there was no pain reflected in their depths. William smirked, "I guess I should have stayed down." Another thud from down the hallway had them trembling in their boots.

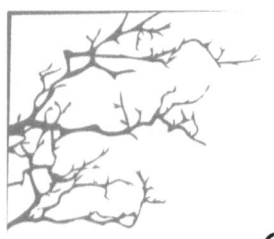

Chapter Thirteen

Scout stared at the house with disbelieving eyes. It was enormous. A lot bigger than the house Force and April were purchasing.

The house sounded like it was groaning. Scout wasn't sure of the reason but surmised it may have experienced growing pains like some of the children she'd saved over the years. She figured if she had grown that big that quickly, she would be making some noises, too.

She would never have imagined a situation such as this. A monstrous building had just eaten two of the local kids. Sucked them inside like a Hoover, and swallowed them whole. She had no idea where Briella was. The assumption was that she was still inside, but without seeing that with her own two eyes, she couldn't be one hundred percent sure. The problem was, the house had refused her entry.

No matter how hard she pushed against the door, it wouldn't budge. She couldn't enter through the holes in the glass because there seemed to be an invisible barrier put in place. "Briella!" she yelled, hoping to get an answer. She was met with the sounds of the house settling into its foundations.

Scout flew from window to window, in search of an entry point. She felt like the house was watching her movements and took great delight in putting obstacles in her way. While fluttering outside one of the upper windows, movement inside caught her eye. Scout's eyes widened with the knowledge she could see the interior of the house. It was like a light switch had been turned on. Glancing at the other windows showed they were back-lit, too. "That's not possible!" Scout yelled at the house. "What is going on?"

Time for reinforcements. She didn't want to contact Force, but this was an emergency. He would be annoyed to have his date interrupted. She would need to make it up to him and April at a later time. Briella was missing, and William and Donovan were stuck inside the house.

THE HOUSE OF HORRORS

The view inside the windows had Scout's blood running cold. The lid on the coffin was opening outwards. Scout wanted to turn away but was rooted to the spot. Her wings fluttered furiously while her breath came in short gasps.

Everything was happening in slow motion. The hand that gripped the lid was white as snow. The arm was covered in the dark sleeve of a jacket with the white cuff of a shirt poking through the bottom. "No," Scout groaned, as little by little the vampire was revealed. "The children."

She could see a shadow creeping along the wall. It was bony and misshapen. Scout squinted her eyes, attempting to locate the source. Could it be the werewolf moving about in there? The shadow crouched then launched across the room. The physical form crossed the window scaring the life out of Scout. It was the werewolf, and it was loping towards the coffin. There was going to be an altercation. What would the victor do when it discovered the prisoners in the house?

Scout swore when the phone went to voice mail for the third time. "What's the point of having a phone if it's turned off?" she screamed into the darkness. Scout flew down to the bottom level and peered into the windows. Briella had to be in there somewhere or else she would have made her presence known. She would not leave the children to fend for themselves. Scout dialled again, but this time left a message. Hopefully, Force and April would arrive sooner rather than later.

Scout kept looking for a way in then remembered the chimney. She could make like Santa and sneak in that way. She reached the opening and found her entrance stopped by an invisible barrier. Scout flew to the front porch and sat on the top step. She needed to find a way in, but to do that, she needed to work out how the house had changed from what she had created to this.

The obvious solution was that Briella's magic had been released somehow. That explained the house's ability to keep her out when she desperately wanted to get in. She wasn't sure how or why the building's size had changed so drastically in the last few minutes. Nor did she have a clue how it was able to drag the kids inside when they were standing metres away. What she did know was that answers had to be found quickly because the creatures upstairs were dangerous and wouldn't remain separated from the kids forever.

'Where are you, Briella?' she thought. 'Please don't take too long to check your messages, Force.'

The sound of footsteps crunching on gravel sent Scout into a panic. She fell off the top step and would have sprained her ankle had her wings not leapt into action. Thankful for the darkness, she flew to the doorframe and landed on top. Hoping the boys would have better luck escaping, she paced impatiently along the top as she waited for the new arrival to come into view.

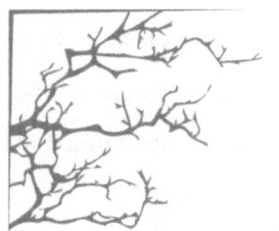

Chapter Fourteen

Things were heating up on the top floor area. The vampire and werewolf were fighting for supremacy. They could smell the scent of prey wafting up the stairs, and neither was willing to share. They were evenly matched in strength and speed, but where the werewolf had four large canines, the vampire had only two fangs.

The nails on the vampire were impressive; long, pointed pieces of keratin that resembled shards of broken glass. The werewolf's claws, however, were like miniature hooks, ready to sink into the flesh of its prey and rip it from the body. The only thing keeping the vampire in the race was the sheer determination of an addict to get its next fix.

The vampire launched the werewolf into the air, impaling it on the bed of nails. The wolf howled in anger, casting a glance down looking for injuries before peeling itself away from the metal spikes. Once it was on its feet, the vampire screamed its rage to see the beast was uninjured. There should have been extensive injuries, but there were no holes and no blood. Before the werewolf could retaliate, the vampire took off for the staircase.

The second the vampire moved, the werewolf understood what the vampire was up to and launched its pursuit. There was no better incentive to win than to have the prey right in front of them. The smell alone would send them into a fighting frenzy.

The boys heard the thumping along the ceiling and quivered with fear. As the sounds became louder and the thuds got closer to the stairs, they decided to move further into the house despite the noises coming from further along. "Okay William, wake up now."

"Stop it, William. That is not helping. Look for something we can use as a weapon."

"What about that lantern over there? It's got fire inside that we might be able to use to scare off whoever is in the house with us."

"Good, go get it, William. I'll look for something we can use as a medieval torch. Hopefully, it won't burn down as fast as a match does."

"I think torches have special stuff coated on them to make them burn slowly."

"Yeah, you're probably right. Holy shit!" William screamed as he got his first glimpse of the werewolf. He hooked his arm around Donovan's chest and pushed him behind.

"What are you doing saying a word like that? Stop pushing me," Donovan struggled.

"I am trying to protect my little brother," William gasped, holding the lantern in front of him like a shield.

The werewolf advanced confidently, licking its lips at the thought of its first meal. It was a few metres away when it was flung to the side to punch a hole in the wall. "What the . . .?" The vampire smiled, and the boys gasped. "Vampire!"

"Dinner," he replied.

With super speed, he was behind William, one arm around his waist while the other tipped his head to the side. He was about to sink his teeth into

THE HOUSE OF HORRORS

William's neck when Donovan reached between the vampire's legs and squeezed tightly. At the same time, the front door opened to reveal the Gatherers.

Force swept into the room, quickly followed by April. Scout had tried to hitch a ride but was sent flying by an invisible force the moment her skin touched the doorway. 'It must have something to do with the house recognising the fairy dust inside me,' she thought.

Scout was extremely frustrated to be left out in the cold with limited access to what was going on inside, and the lack of ability for her to provide help. She made her way back to the frame above the door and plonked herself on the edge. There was no point in getting herself riled up by what was going on inside. Better to wait and hear what happened rather than watching it unfold and be annoyed.

"I wouldn't do that if I were you," Force stated with a fireball in each palm.

The vampire hesitated for a second then began to slowly lower his head, testing Force's resolve.

Force sent a stream of fire in the vampire's direction, stopping a metre short. The heat was enough to cause discomfort to all parties. The vampire let go with a hiss and retreated into the kitchen. By this time, the werewolf had gotten to its feet and had stepped back through the hole in the wall. It was unnaturally quiet, sneaking up on its prey rather than howling its pre-victory song.

William was focused on Donovan, trying to prevent him from going into shock. Force was chasing down the vampire, which left April to deal with the werewolf. "Hey, Bozo. You want a piece of this?" she called, transforming herself into a female version of it.

The boys looked at her with wide eyes. Donovan said to William, "Are you seeing this?"

"Hmmm, Hmmm," he answered.

"How many of those mushrooms did we eat?" Donovan asked.

"Too many," he replied, squeezing himself even closer to his brother.

The werewolf turned and launched himself at April. She was ready for him. Her claws came out as she showed off her canines. She dug her claws into his flesh as he knocked her off her feet. His canines sank into her shoulder, ripping some of her flesh as they landed in a heap on the floor. Her wound instantly knitted together while she dragged the claws on her uninjured side through his body. Blood poured over her until his body began healing itself.

She got her legs under him and hefted him off her. His body sailed through the air, hitting the force field that surrounded the openings of the building. His body was thrown back in her direction at the same time the boys let out another shriek.

A mummy had its hand wrapped around Donovan's neck and he was quickly running out of air. William was attempting to unwind the bandage, but it kept doing itself up again. "If we live through this, Donovan, we are never eating mushrooms again, and we are going to leave other people's rubbish where we found it."

Donovan's face turned purple before he lost consciousness.

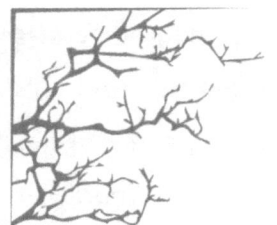

Chapter Fifteen

Briella was hurting. She raised her hand and felt the lump that had risen on the right-hand side of her head. She lifted herself onto hands and knees, nearly flopping forward as a woozy feeling settled over her.

"Scout?" she groaned, hoping her friend was near.

Briella swallowed the saliva that was tainting her mouth, hoping she wouldn't lose the contents of her stomach. She waited a few seconds for her head to stop spinning before gingerly getting to an upright position. The light hurt her eyes.

She heard the sounds of fighting around her, but couldn't seem to make head nor tail of what was happening. Briella blinked a few times in an attempt to allow her eyes to adjust to the light. It didn't help. The massive egg on her head indicated a pretty serious head injury. With any luck, it wasn't something that would cause permanent damage.

She felt the rush of wind as the werewolf sailed past her. Her eyes opened wide in surprise before the brightness caused her to squint. 'Was that my werewolf?' she thought. 'No it couldn't have been.' She shook her head then wished she hadn't. April's voice was familiar but different. It had taken on a gravelly tone. Briella closed her eyes and sent out the strongest signal she could muster. 'April!'

"Briella? Where are you?" April grunted as the werewolf ploughed into her, knocking her over.

'I'm stuck inside my drawing,' she replied through mind-link.

"Oh, love, we are all stuck inside your drawing," April told her.

'Who?'

"The twins, Liam and myself. Your creatures are running around trying to kill them. In fact, a mummy has got one of the twins by the neck and is bound to kill him unless you do something."

'What can I do without my magic?' Briella thought.

"Try ordering it to stop. You are its creator, Briella. Maybe it has to do what you tell it to, just like Frankenstein's monster."

Briella flew closer to the boys, yelling at the mummy to stop. To her surprise, it did, allowing Donovan to fall through its fingers. "Holy crap!" she cried, holding her head between her hands from the pain. '*It worked, April.*'

"Great, can you do the same with all the creatures in the building now?"

'*Sure,*' she replied, '*but I don't know how long I can hold them. My head is about to split open.*'

"I don't think you have to constantly control them. Giving them an instruction should be all you'd need to do."

"Beings of the house, I command you to stop hurting the living."

The creatures, wherever they were at that moment, dropped to the floor and started to howl with rage. The house itself seemed to feel the pain of its inhabitants, the wood groaning in sympathy. Force came looking for April to discuss the strange behaviour of the vampire when the front door opened and a group of adults walked into the foyer.

Force swore under his breath and morphed into a living statue in the shape of a gargoyle. The last thing he needed was for the townspeople to discover him mixed up in weird stuff. He wanted them to trust him, not be wary of him. As Force's thoughts were sitting on the surface, April was able to pick them up while her mind-link was open. She followed suit and morphed into a living statue of a dragon.

The group consisted of two women and three men. None of them was familiar to the Gatherers, but they seemed to be known to the boys. Briella sent out a new command, "Creatures of the house, you must remain still and quiet."

The adults wandered further into the building, stopping to chat briefly with the twins. Donovan had regained consciousness but was still looking rather dark in the face. William rose to his feet. "Please help us. We ate some funny mushrooms and are in the middle of a hallucination. Can you wake us up or something?"

"How about you run along home, boys? Your parents will be starting to wonder what the pair of you are up to."

"We can't leave the house."

"Don't be ridiculous," a gruff looking male stated. "You get up and walk out that door and don't stop anywhere until you get home. I'll let your folks know you are on your way."

William helped Donovan rise to his feet. Together they walked to the door left open by the latest invaders, prepared to be bounced back into the room. The house didn't hurt the children but held the barrier in place so they couldn't pass.

"Oh for Heaven's sake," gruff man said, storming towards the boys. He placed his hands on their backs and shoved them hard. William and Donovan turned their faces to the side to stop their noses from breaking. They weren't too sure whether their cheeks would withstand the pressure.

"Stop!" they cried.

The man pulled them back and tried to step through himself, without success. "What the Hell?"

THE HOUSE OF HORRORS

"You are in our hallucination now," William stated. "Stuck here like the rest of us."

"Who else is in here with you?"

"Force and April, our newest residents."

"Never heard of them."

"Did you hear about the missing kids?" Donovan asked.

"Yep."

"Well, Force and April are the ones who found them and returned them safely."

"So where are they now?"

"I don't know. They were here just a minute ago."

"Let's see if we can find them and find out what is going on?"

"We already told you what is going on. You are stuck in our dream."

"Don't be ridiculous," gruff man said. "We just finished a lovely dinner at the Pub. This place wasn't here when we arrived. So, for starters, I'd like to know how a two-storey establishment was put together in just a few hours. Then I'd like to find out how the building is able to prevent us from leaving."

"I'm guessing you ate the same mushrooms we did and somehow we are all stuck in the same dream," William said.

"There weren't any mushrooms in our meal, son. Even if there were, they wouldn't be the kind to make a person believe in something that wasn't real."

"Then, how do you explain all of this?" Donovan asked, waving his arms around.

"Got to be some kind of magic. Someone has been creating a surprise for Halloween and has somehow discovered how to keep it hidden from the public."

William and Donovan glanced at one another. "Did he just say magic?" William asked Donovan who nodded his head. "This dude is crazier than both our imaginations put together."

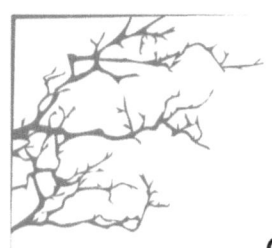

Chapter Sixteen

Briella had smelled mushrooms on the boys as they passed her position. If she could secure some, it would help to heal her lumps and bumps. She was formulating a plan when the other adults returned from their exploration of the house.

"James, you've got to see this place. It would make for a fantastic Halloween party. The statues in this place are so life-like, it's a pity they don't move. Imagine the terror this place could create. People would talk about it for years to come."

"It wasn't here a few hours ago, Jane. Something is not right here. The house won't even let us leave."

"Don't be ridiculous," she laughed, smoothing out the lines on her face and making the skin around her eyes wrinkle.

While they were talking, Briella had a great idea. She could use this house as the base for her surprise party. Now that she knew she could control the creatures, she could reanimate them on All Hallow's Eve and give the townsfolk a night to remember. They could be frightened out of their wits, with no fear on Briella's part of them being injured. With the extra people in the house, she decided to test out her theory, but first, she needed to heal.

She fluttered over to the twins and picked William's pocket. They were so busy watching the interchange between James and Jane and trying to keep an eye on the werewolf, that they didn't even notice her.

Within minutes, Briella felt well enough to test out her idea. She ventured to each monster contained within the building, including Force and April, and whispered her plan into their ears. Then she flew to the nearest chandelier to watch the events unfold.

The werewolf rose to his feet as did the mummy. The twins eyes widened in fear before a determined look crossed their faces. The movement of the creatures had caught the attention of the adults in the room. Their reaction attracted the notice of the monsters. William and Donovan took the opportunity to run into the guest bedroom and hid beneath the bed. They were ecstatic to discover they had the space to themselves, fearing a bogeyman would be waiting for them.

Jane's face became animated with excitement. "They do move," she squealed with delight, gripping her hands together. "I wonder what they do?" She didn't have to wait long. The werewolf pounced on her, knocking her to the ground. He was faster than she had expected and fear soon crept into her features.

The werewolf glared at her with hungry yellow eyes. His teeth were bared and pictures of him ripping out her throat fluttered behind her eyelids. Drool hung from his bottom lip. One flick of his head would have it splattering all over her face. Her hands were raised in a protective

115

position, but she realised he was far superior in strength to her.

Jane's first thought was how glad she was to have gone to the toilet before they left the pub. Otherwise, she would have peed herself by now. Her second thought was that she shouldn't have wished the statues could move. It might have been better had she wanted them to merely growl or something as they walked past.

The third thought was that without help, she might die tonight in a house filled with terrifying creatures which could disappear at any moment, with their decaying bodies trapped inside. There would be no insight into their gruesome end, and they would quickly become a cold case. "James!" she screamed, hoping he would offer her some assistance.

He couldn't help. James was busy with his own problems. The mummy had scooped him up under its arms and was carrying him up the stairs. This was quite a feat considering James was well over two metres tall and weighed in excess of one hundred kilograms. The harder he struggled, the tighter the mummy's grip, reminding him of a boa constrictor.

He decided to wait and see where the mummy took him and then he would come up with a plan for escape. There was nothing he could do while he was still in the mummy's hold.

The adults in other areas of the house were being hunted by the creatures. The other female found herself captured by the vampire who was toying with her emotions. The smallest male of the group, standing at one hundred and sixty centimetres and weighing seventy kilograms had been snafued by a club-wielding ogre that had been engrossed in cataloguing the contents of the walk-in pantry. The other male found himself chained to the wall upstairs with a bogeyman intent on using some of his body parts as meat for the stew he was cooking over a blazing fire pit.

Briella touched the walls of the house and whispered to it, "I would like to use you for my Halloween party, but to do that, people will need to be able to enter and leave. I would like for you to offer them a thrill of a lifetime, but they need to be able to exit to tell their friends to come to you."

She could feel the house pulsing as it processed her request. Briella wasn't sure how to test whether the house was accepting of her appeal. If she managed to leave, she wasn't sure if the house would let her back in and she needed to be inside to keep an eye on the creatures. She would just have to wait until Force and April sprang into action 'to save the day', and see if the house would let the humans leave.

Force moved down the hallway, following the path the vampire took. He knew the creature wouldn't bite his victim, but there were other unsavoury characteristics that vampires had at their disposal. He wanted to make sure the vampire hadn't charmed his victim and was making her do something against her will.

April spread her wings as far as the walls would allow and growled at the werewolf. It turned its head in her direction without letting go of Jane.

"You've done your job and given her a scare, now it is time to let her go."

"I don't think so," he replied, the voice sending shivers of excitement up her spine. Damned if she wasn't attracted to a figment of Briella's imagination. "Briella wants the victims to be terrified, and this one's heart has only risen forty beats. Another forty and I will let her go."

The werewolf turned its attention back to Jane and lowered its head towards her throat. His teeth got within a few centimetres, the slobber leaving a trail across her skin. April knocked the beast off Jane and pushed him into a corner. She then shouted at Jane to head for the front door. Jane didn't need to be told twice. She ran out of there as fast as her legs would take her, then whooped with delight. "That was awesome!" her voice could be heard yelling, now that the danger had passed.

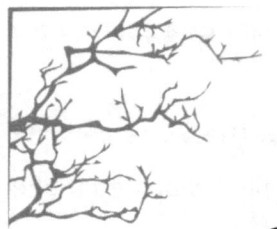

Chapter Seventeen

The vampire had its victim secured firmly in a corner. The woman was facing away from the vampire, her cheek lying flush against the wall. Her wrists were tightly secured behind her back in one of his hands while his other gently brushed the hair away from the left-hand side of her neck.

"You smell so good, I could eat you up," he crooned, bringing his nose close to the skin and taking a whiff.

Force could hear her whimpers of terror from the doorway. "Leave her be, Abomination."

"Why should I? I'm a vampire, and she's food." He grabbed her hair and yanked her head back, exposing her neck further. He spun them around, so the woman was between Force and himself. "Look how quickly her pulse beats for me. Listen to the whimpers of anticipation streaming from her throat."

"They are the sounds of fear you are listening to, you sadistic monster," Force replied, advancing on his prey.

"You cannot hurt me, Gargoyle, for I am immortal."

"You, my friend, are not real. You are merely a figment of the imagination of an overzealous fairy."

"I am losing my mind," the young woman stated, closing her eyes tightly and praying that she woke up from her nightmare soon.

"You will lose your power at sunrise and return to a flattened state," Force said.

"Then I had better stop listening to the little one and have what fun I can before it is taken away from me completely."

"You are here to provide entertainment to the humans, not to cause them bodily harm. They wish to celebrate a most terrifying time of the year and who better to scare them than a glorified vampire such as yourself."

"That is true," he replied as he gently stroked the woman's neck with his claw.

"And that will end if you kill her. There will be nobody left to fear you, and you will have failed in your duty."

"Well we can't have that, can we?"

"Definitely not."

"So what do you propose I do?"

"Let her go so that you may continue hunting. If she is not quick enough to exit, you can catch her once more. Of course, it would be more fun to find another victim to terrorise."

"I don't know," the vampire said, "seeing the shocked look on her face as I snatched her up into my arms again would be a more than adequate outcome to the hunt."

"So maybe you could give her a head start."

"That would be satisfactory." He turned to the woman, "You've got to the count of twenty before I come for you. Go quickly, or you will find yourself in a situation that is pleasing to me but not perhaps for yourself."

She stood still for a few seconds, so he counted out loud. "Five, six . . ."

The woman took off, running into a chair and bruising her hip in her haste to get away. Force blocked the vampire's route, ensuring the woman's getaway. He just hoped that Briella was successful in convincing the house to let them go.

When he heard her laughter of joy, Force assumed she had made it and stepped back into the hallway. He listened carefully and discovered movement on the upstairs level. He was racing for the stairs when a crash in the kitchen caught his attention.

Force skidded to a halt and reversed direction. He arrived at the entrance to find a man cowering beneath a table with the ogre preparing to decimate the structure with its club. "Wait!" Force yelled. "The table might splinter and cut the human. If it nicks an artery, he will bleed out, and the meat will become tough."

"Me an ogre. Me not likes the meat. Me only eats them bones."

"Well I like the meat," Force said in a confrontational tone as he moved towards the table, "and I don't like my meat tough."

"This is my food," the ogre yelled. "Find your own."

"Why should I when you waste the best bits? We should share." Force's tail swooped in under the table and grabbed the guy around the chest, pinning his arms to his sides. He flung him outside the room before the scream could escape him. Once the dizziness had passed from the speed of movement, he headed towards the door only to find himself snaffled by the vampire. "Well, well, well. What have we here?"

Force's voice came down the hallway. "Fine, you have him then. I'll go find my own."

Force ran out of the room and skidded to a halt. 'Poor guy is never going to leave his house again,' he thought. "Hello again, vampire. I see you've found another victim."

"Indeed, and this one is way more frightened than the female." His claws gently stroked the neck of his prey. "Look how the blood rushes away from the skin, leaving him pale."

"You are going to scare him to death."

"That would be a let-down now, wouldn't it?"

"Perhaps you had better find a more suitable victim to play with," Force suggested.

"Fine," the vampire pouted, listening for other heartbeats. "Seems like the party's moved upstairs." He was gone in the blink of an eye. The ogre came bursting out of the kitchen in search of the man, swinging the club above his head as he screamed with rage.

"You'd better run for the door quickly," Force advised, turning to face the ogre head-on.

The guy looked as though he was going to pass out. Force was about to scoop him up and run him outside when Jane arrived, grabbing him by the hand. "Come on, Spud, let's get you home."

"Yes, I think I need a lie-down. It's been a very long day, and I think I got a little too much sun."

"I need you to come quickly, Spud. Can you do that?"

"No, I think I am going to be sick."

Jane pulled him along behind her, trying desperately to quench the fear that was threatening to overwhelm her. Force shoulder charged the ogre, without making a dent in the beast's advance. "You puny creature. No match for ogre," he said reaching a hand out to push him to the side. "Me wants bones."

"You can't have them," Force replied, wrapping his tail around a leg and using the big guy's weight against him. He fell to the floor with a thud, causing the house to shudder. The ogre had barely missed taking Spud out with his head as it charged towards the floor.

Spud's hand tore out of Jane's as he spun around with a hand over his heart. His vision went dark for a second before he felt the calming touch of Jane's hand on his shoulder. "It's over now. Let's get you home."

"I don't like Halloween, Jane. Please don't expect me to escort you to any of the parties that you have been invited to."

"It's fine, Spud. We'll just have a quiet one at home and watch some Christmas movies."

THE HOUSE OF HORRORS

"Christmas, yeah I'd like that," he replied as she turned him around and walked him out the door.

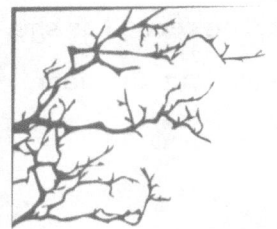

Chapter Eighteen

Scout flew in through the door with relief that she was finally being given admittance. She had tried to enter when she saw the girls exit the building, but it wasn't until Spud had stepped over the threshold that she was able to pass through the barrier.

Briella saw her enter and swooped down to give her a mid-air hug. "Oh, Scout. I am so glad you are here. Where have you been?"

"Stuck outside, roosting like a chicken."

"Pardon?"

"Your house wouldn't let me in. I've been going out of my mind imagining all sorts of things going on inside these walls. Is everybody safe? What about April and Force? Are they all right?"

"Everybody is fine, Scout. Settle down a bit." Briella flew her upstairs to see what was going on.

April had placed her dragon body between the man chained to the wall and the bogeyman who was looking forward to some ear of man soup. Scout admired the bluish-green scales that covered her body. "Oh, Briella. She's beautiful. That would have to be my favourite creation so far."

Briella burst into fits of laughter. "That's April," she managed to get out between cackles.

"Why is she a dragon?"

"She and Liam are testing out a plan for me. I'm thinking of using this as the base for our Halloween party. We have discovered that the creatures have to do as I say, and I have told them they cannot cause physical harm to the humans. They can, however, give them the fright of their lives."

"How is that possible? John and the other pumpkins didn't listen to your commands. What makes these ones different?"

"They are my own creations. The pumpkins were already alive before they received my magic. That seems to be the thing that makes the difference."

"So what is going on here, then?"

"The Gatherers are going to appear to save the day from the baddies which will hopefully alleviate some of the humans' unease when they finally become free and think about the unnatural events that have occurred in here. I am hoping they will find themselves thinking about this place the same way they would a roller coaster or some other frightening situation. Terrified at the time it is happening, but longing for some more when the ride is over."

"The Gatherers will never go for it. Besides, the party was to be a surprise for them."

"By the way they've been behaving, I think they are having as much fun as the women who recently escaped. I caught a glimpse of Liam's thoughts, and I think he is planning on asking me to make this happen again on All Hallow's Eve. He is going to invite the town to experience the House of Horrors."

They watched as April freed the man and carefully gripped him by her teeth and threw him over her head to hang on to her neck for dear life. She ran awkwardly towards the staircase, with him nestled on her back and the bogeyman racing behind her to recapture him. Force had encased the mummy in a force field, encouraging James to head for the front door. He wasted no time in leaving, heading for the back door to keep out of sight from the bogeyman who was following April towards the front door.

Once the adults were gone, April and Force morphed into their natural forms. They fell into each other's arms, laughing with pleasure. "That was fantastic," Liam said.

"Oh, Liam. That was so much fun. We should do it again, now that we know they won't hurt the people."

"You're forgetting one thing. This will all cease to exist once the sun rises."

"Briella can sprinkle her magic again to bring them to life."

"Are you sure that is a good idea? Her magic will be so much stronger then. Perhaps she won't have the same amount of control over the creatures the closer to Halloween we get."

"It's worth the risk, April. These people are going to be our neighbours. I'd like to give them something special."

"You could do that with your other gifts, Liam. You don't need to use Briella to make yourself look good."

"That was not my intention," he stalked off towards the kitchen.

Scout flew over and landed on his shoulder. "Why is this so important to you?"

"It is important for Briella."

"In what way?"

"She has spent years trying to hide what she sees as a fault with her magic at Halloween."

"You've got to admit, it does create some unique situations."

"Precisely. Imagine the boost she would feel if her wacky magic was used to bring some fun to the town. She might never again need to feel bad at this time of year."

Donovan appeared by their side. "If you could re-create this for Halloween, you would be the talk of the town."

"I thought you were hallucinating?" Force questioned.

"I am. I watched you change into a gargoyle and back. I am talking to a fairy who is perched on your shoulder. I know I am feeling the effects of the mushrooms we ate from the forest before checking if it was safe to do so. That doesn't mean I wouldn't like to see something like this that we could explore and be frightened by for Halloween. Some of the city kids I skype with talk about the Haunted Houses at the fairs they attend. They have so much fun being frightened, they nearly wet their pants."

"Let's get you guys home," Force said, placing his hand on the boy's shoulder.

"Yeah, we should probably sleep this off."

"A good meal would go a long way to neutralising the effects of the mushrooms," Force replied.

"I think I might stay here. What if somebody else enters the building?" Scout said.

"I think we've had enough fun for one night. Why don't you shrink it to a size that can be easily carried? The monsters can have fun with each other until sunrise. Then you can change them back to paper form and store them safely for Halloween."

"Yeah, I can do that. Let's get out of here."

The group left the building with a pang of disappointment that their adventure had ended. They did have a flutter of excitement that they might be able to do this again on a larger scale, and with more people to protect from the scary creatures.

The boys were escorted home safely, their parents pleased to find them in the care of Force and April. They were beginning to worry that their boys might have been kidnapped. Force assured their parents that their children were perfectly safe and promised that no more kids would go missing while on his watch. April and Force declined a quick drink before they left. It was then that they realised they hadn't eaten their dinner.

"Let's go back to the pub and make some toasted cheese sandwiches," said April.

"Only if you agree to go to the Devil's Gate for dinner with me tomorrow night," replied Force.

While Liam and April were talking together, Briella and Scout were whispering to each other, making sure to protect their thoughts from eavesdropping Gatherers. "We should test your control over magically affected things further, Briella."

"What do you mean?"

"We know you can't control things that were already living, but you can control sketches that were brought to life. What if we tried to make something from inanimate objects and bring that to life, like Frankenstein's monster, but not with tissue that was once alive."

"What did you have in mind?"

"I think we should make a scarecrow."

Briella felt the shiver that ran through her body at the mention of the one thing that frightened the life out of her. "I'd rather not do that," Briella stated.

"Why not? It would be perfect. We can get some clothes and stuff them with straw. Then you can sprinkle your dust, and we can laugh as it chases the crows away for real."

"What if it decides to chase the humans instead?" 'Or fairies?' That thought was kept to herself.

"It won't, but if it does, we will destroy it."

"I don't know," Briella murmured.

"We'll sleep on it," Scout said excitedly, her eyes glowing with mischief.

"That is, if these two can stay out of mischief for one evening," Liam aimed his comment at the two fairies.

Scout hooked her arm around Briella's and smiled all the way home.

Titles by Marnie Atwell

Starlight Investigations

Jealousy Monsters

Vampire

Phantasm

Halloween Madness

The Pumpkin Patch

The House of Horrors

The Spirited Scarecrow

The Curious Kitten

About the Author

Marnie is an Australian author who lives in South-East Queensland with her husband and two children. When she is not dreaming up new adventures for her characters; Marnie enjoys writing, reading paranormal romance novels, and spending time with her family and friends. Not necessarily in that order.

Visit her website at: www.marnieatwell.com for more books, pictures, and downloads.

The next book in this series is:

The Spirited Scarecrow